Jim Aylesworth's

Book of

BEDTIME STORIES

Jim Aylesworth's

Book of

BEDTIME

STORIES

by JIM AYLESWORTH

illustrated by EILEEN CHRISTELOW,
JO ELLEN McALLISTER-STAMMEN,
and WALTER LYON KRUDOP

ATHENEUM BOOKS FOR YOUNG READERS

Atheneum Books for Young Readers
An imprint of Simon & Schuster Children's Publishing Division
1230 Avenue of the Americas
New York, New York 10020

Book design by Nina Barnett

First Edition

Printed in Hong Kong

10 9 8 7 6 5 4 3 2 1

Library of Congress Catalog Card Number 97-77744
ISBN 0-689-82077-1

Contents

dear adults,

Wouldn't it be nice if the children in our lives remembered us fondly even when they're age ninety-two going on ninety-three?

Then let's read to them now. Let's read to them every day. Pleasant childhood experiences with books are never forgotten.

Wouldn't you like to enrich their lives and instill in them a love of literature?

Let's read to them now; read to them every day.

Wouldn't you like for them to be excited about learning to read, and wouldn't you like for them to do better in school all around?

I know I don't even need to ask. So let's read to our children now, every day.

And wouldn't you want to help them settle into sleep each night, happy and hopeful and secure?

Let's read bedtime stories. Let's read them every night. Bedtime stories are written just for that purpose. There are many to chose from, and here you have chosen four of mine. They are my way of saying to you and to yours, "Good night. I care."

With love!

Jim Aylesworth

Two Terrible Frights

Modeling the skills of good parents, the mothers in this fantasy distract their children and give them something interesting to think about as they fall asleep.

J.A.

Two Terrible Frights

written by JIM AYLESWORTH

illustrated by EILEEN CHRISTELOW

ONCE UPON A TIME, there was
a big old farm house, way out in the country.

Downstairs, in the basement, in a cozy corner, a little mouse was thinking about a bedtime snack.

And upstairs, in a cozy room, a little girl was also thinking about a bedtime snack.

The little mouse went to her mother and said, "Mommy, can I have a snack before I go to bed? Maybe a little piece of cheese?" The little mouse's mother said, "Yes, but you'll have to go up to the kitchen and get it for yourself. I've been working all day, and I'm tired."

And at just about the very same moment, the little girl went to her mother and said, "Mommy, can I have a snack before I go to bed? Maybe a little glass of milk?" The little girl's mother said, "Yes, but you'll have to go down to the kitchen and get it for yourself. I've been at work all day, and I'm tired."

The little mouse said, "I can't go up there all by myself! There might be a monster or something just waiting to get me!" The little mouse's mother said, "Don't be silly."

The little girl said, "I can't go down there all by myself! There might be a creature or something that'll jump out and get me!" The little girl's mother said, "How ridiculous."

So, the little mouse started for the kitchen,
all by herself,
. . . quietly up the radiator pipe,
. . . tiptoe under the floor . . .

. . . through a dark hole,

. . . under the stove,

. . . and out across the kitchen floor.

And at just about the very same moment, the little girl
also started for the kitchen, all by herself,
. . . quietly down the long hall,
. . . tiptoe down the stairs . . .

. . . through the dark parlor,
. . . through the dining room,
. . . and into the kitchen.

And just when the little mouse was right in the middle of the floor, the little girl flipped on the light.

CLICK

They both stood very very still, and looked at each other.

Then, at just about the very same moment, the little mouse went "SQUEAK!", and the little girl went "EEEK!", and they both took off running!

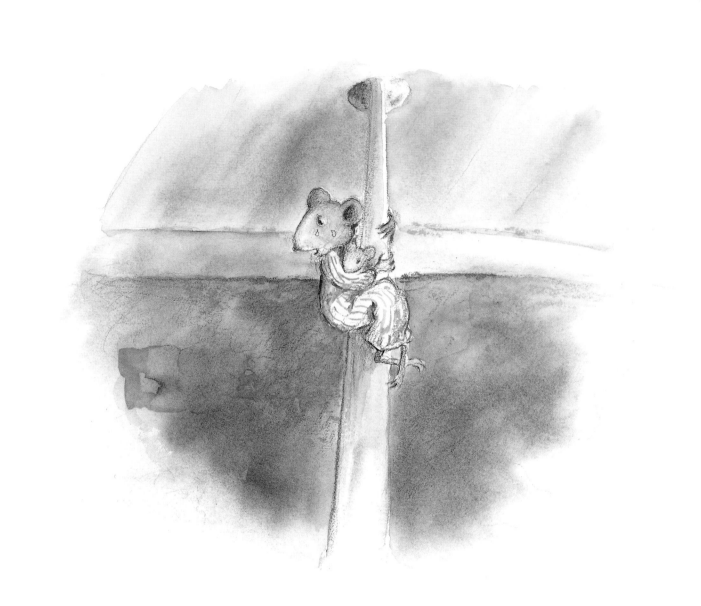

The little mouse ran back under the stove, back down the hole, back under the floor, back down the radiator pipe, all the while hollering, "Mommy! Mommy! Mommy!"

And just as fast, the little girl ran back through the dining room, back through the parlor, back up the stairs, back down the hallway, all the while hollering, "Mommy! Mommy! Mommy!"

The little mouse sobbed, "There was a person up there, and it 'eeeked' at me."

The little girl sobbed, "There was a mouse down there, and it 'squeaked' at me."

"Now, now, now," said the little mouse's mother. "I can tell that you've had a terrible fright, but I'll bet that person you saw was a little girl person, and you probably scared her worse than she scared you."

"Now, now, now," said the little girl's mother. "I can tell that you've had a terrible fright, but I'll just bet that mouse you saw was a little girl mouse, and you probably scared her worse than she scared you."

"Do you really think so?" said the little mouse, drying her tears and crawling into bed. "I hope I didn't scare her too bad." "I'm sure she'll get over it," said the little mouse's mother. Then she kissed her on the cheek and said goodnight.

"Do you really think so?" said the little girl, drying her tears and crawling into bed. "I hope I didn't scare her too bad." "I'm sure she'll get over it," said the little girl's mother. Then, she kissed her on the cheek and said goodnight.

The little mouse fell asleep in her soft bed, thinking about the little girl.

And at just about the very same moment, the little girl fell asleep in her soft bed, thinking about the little mouse.

And they both dreamed . . .

. . . about each other.

Teddy Bear Tears

The sweet child in this story knows just how to ease the fears of his teddy bears, and I know where he learned how to do it. Someday, I know for sure that he will be as skillful with his own real live children.

J.A.

Teddy Bear
Tears

written by JIM AYLESWORTH

illustrated by JO ELLEN McALLISTER-STAMMEN

There once was a boy who had four teddy bears.

Their names were Willie Bear, Fuzzy, Ringo, and Little Sam.

The little boy loved them
all very much, and every
night they slept together in
a big, cozy bed.

And some nights, there
were tears.

They began as soon as the
lights went out . . . quiet
sniffles. . . .

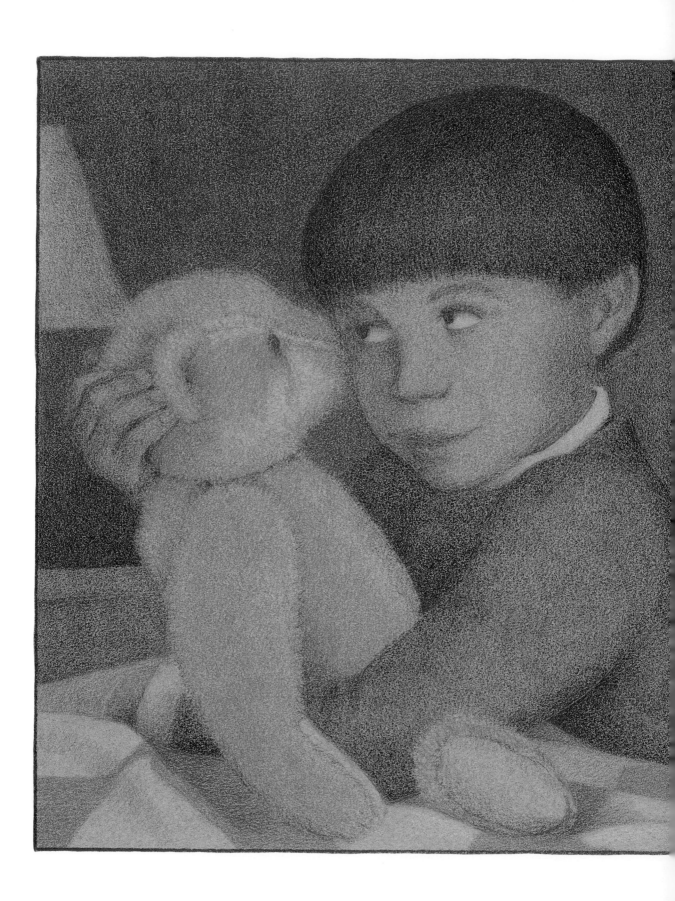

And on this night, they came again.

"Is that you, Willie Bear?" asked the boy as he took Willie Bear into his arms. "Are you crying?"

Willie Bear stopped his sniffling, and with his head up close to the little boy's ear, he whispered in a way that only the little boy could hear. "I heard a scary noise outside the window."

"Don't be scared," said the little boy, getting out of bed and carrying Willie Bear to the window. "See how pretty it is out there in the moonlight? See how the stars shine and how the wind moves the trees?"

Willie Bear nodded.

"Well, that wind makes a noise, but it's nothing to be scared of.

"And sometimes there's a cat out poking around, or maybe a moth bumping against the screen. They make noises, too, but there's nothing out there that would hurt a little bear."

Willie Bear whispered
into the little boy's ear.
"Okay, but can I sleep up
real close to you just in case
I hear something else and
get scared?"

"Sure," said the little boy.
Then he took Willie Bear
back to bed, tucked him up
real close to his side, and
put his arm around him.

For a moment, all was
quiet. Then, little sniffles
came again.

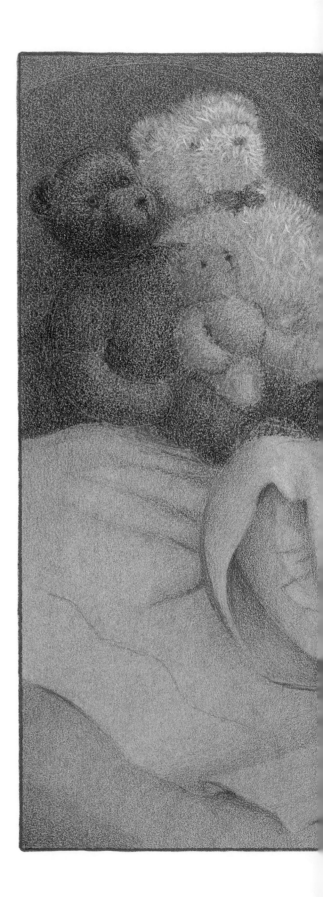

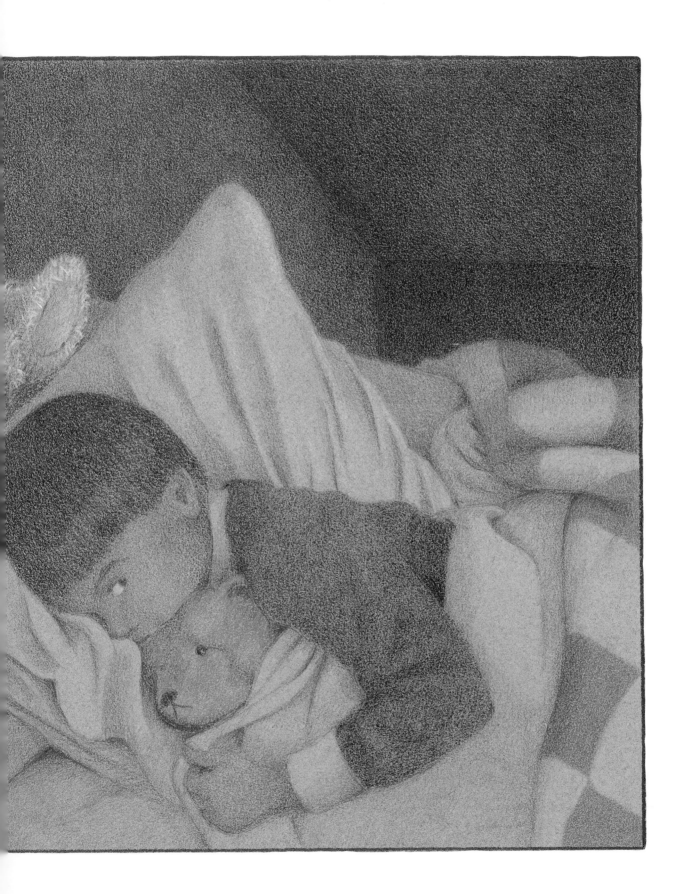

"Is that you, Fuzzy?" The little boy took Fuzzy into his arms and hugged him real close.

Fuzzy stopped his sniffles, and like Willie Bear, he whispered in a way that only the boy could hear. "I'm scared there's something under the bed. Something like an alligator or a cobra or something like that."

"Don't be scared," said the little boy as he turned on the lamp and got down on the floor with Fuzzy in his arms.

"There's nothing under here . . . nothing to be scared of, I mean . . . just an old sock, a piece from one of my puzzles, and lots of dust and stuff. You're not scared of dust, are you?"

"No," whispered Fuzzy. "But just in case, can I sleep up close to you and Willie Bear? I'd feel much better if I did."

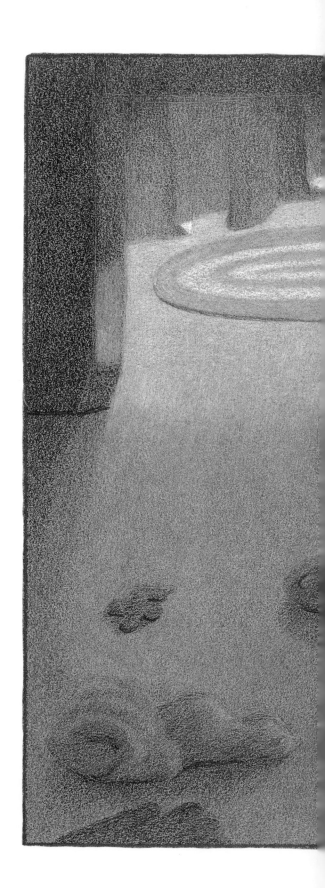

The little boy got back
into bed and turned out the
light.

He tucked Willie Bear up
real close on one side and
Fuzzy up real close on the
other side, and put his arms
around them both.

And for a moment, there
wasn't a sound.

Then the little sniffles
came again.

"Ringo? You too?" He pulled Ringo up into his arms and hugged him tight.

Ringo's furry head was right up next to the boy's ear, and very softly, he whispered, "There's a bogey man in the closet."

"Ringo, you know there is no such thing as a bogey man!" said the little boy, turning on the lamp again and taking Ringo over to the closet.

"And there's nothing in this closet that could hurt you! Just my clothes and shoes and stuff." Then he turned on the closet light so Ringo could get a better look. "Do you see anything scary in here?"

"No," answered Ringo. "But could I sleep up close to you and Willie Bear and Fuzzy anyway? Just in case?"

The little boy climbed back in bed.

He tucked Willie Bear up real close on one side, and Fuzzy up real close on the other side, and he put Ringo up on top. Then, he put his arms around all three and closed his eyes.

But right away, more sniffles started.

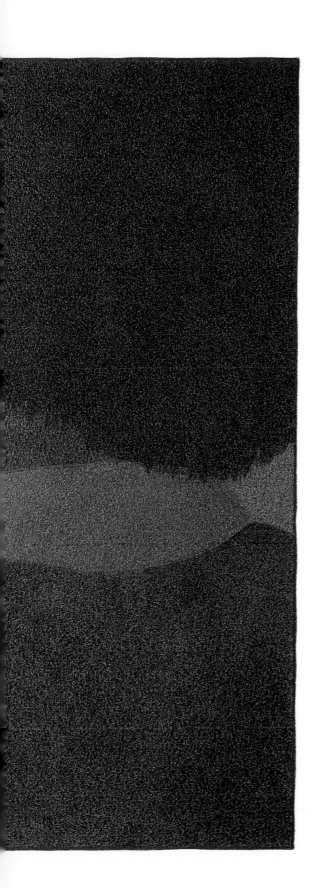

"That has to be you, Little Sam," said the boy.

He reached for Little Sam and hugged him close.

Little Sam whispered into the boy's ear. "It's too dark in here. It scares me to be so dark."

"Oh, Little Sam," said the boy. "There's no reason to be afraid of the dark." He got out of bed, ran across the hall, and flipped on the bathroom light.

When he returned, there was a patch of soft light lying across the end of the bed. "Is that better now?" asked the little boy.

"Yes," whispered Sam. "But can't I sleep up close with you and Willie Bear and Fuzzy and Ringo? Just in case?"

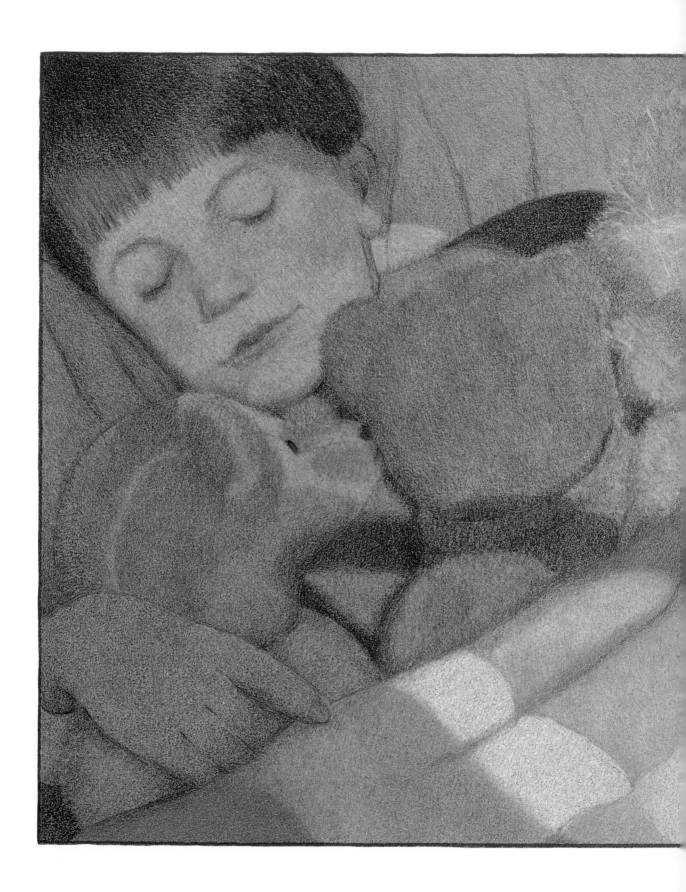

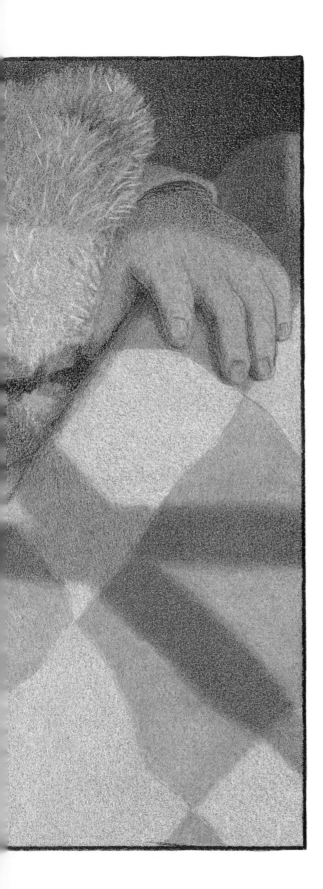

"Sure," said the little boy, and he settled back down on his pillow. He tucked Willie Bear up real close on one side and Fuzzy up real close on the other side. Ringo and Little Sam he put up on top. Then he put his arms around them all.

"Good night, you guys," said the little boy. "I love you."

"We love you, too," said the bears.

And then, after only a moment more, the boy was sound asleep . . .

. . . and dreaming very pleasant dreams.

The Completed
Hickory Dickory Dock

Kevin's day mirrors the active life of any child, and as I read these rhymes, so does my voice; loud at first, and then softer and softer as he settles into sleep. These parents know what they are doing.

J.A.

The Completed
Hickory Dickory Dock

written by **JIM AYLESWORTH**

illustrated by **EILEEN CHRISTELOW**

Hickory, dickory, dock.
The mouse ran up the clock.

The clock struck one,
And down he run.
Hickory, dickory, dock.

Nibble on, bibble on, bees.
The mouse bit off some cheese.
The clock struck two,
Away he flew.
Nibble on, bibble on, bees.

Honeybee, bunny bee, boo.
The mouse ran into a shoe.
The clock struck three,
He scratched a flea.
Honeybee, bunny bee, boo.

Apple eye, dapple eye, day.
The mouse just loves to play.
The clock struck four,
He rolled on the floor.
Apple eye, dapple eye, day.

Milky Way, silky way, sat.
The mouse got chased by a cat.

The clock struck five,
He's glad he's alive.
Milky Way, silky way, sat.

Slippery, whippery, whirl.
The mouse showed off to a girl.
The clock struck six,
He finished his tricks.
Slippery, whippery, whirl.

Chickadee, rickadee, run.
His papa calls him Son.
The clock struck seven,
His real name is Kevin.
Chickadee, rickadee, run.

Icicle, bicycle, bert.
The mouse had pie for dessert.
The clock struck eight,
He licked the plate.
Icicle, bicycle, bert.

Splashery, dashery, dears.
The mouse washed off his ears.
The clock struck nine,
He gave them a shine.
Splashery, dashery, dears.

Peekaboo, teekaboo, took.
His mama read him a book.
The clock struck ten,
She read it again.
Peekaboo, teekaboo, took.

Tippytoe, hippytoe, head.
The mouse knelt by his bed.
The clock struck eleven,
His prayers went to heaven.
Tippytoe, hippytoe, head.

Silvery, bilvery, beams.
The mouse had wonderful dreams.
The clock struck twelve,
Now dream some yourselves.
Silvery, bilvery, beams.

The Good-Night Kiss

The "surprise" at the end of this lulling story is the legacy of every child. I am proud to be the author of a story that invites such an outcome.

J.A.

The Good-Night Kiss

written by JIM AYLESWORTH

illustrated by WALTER LYON KRUDOP

On the night of the good-night kiss, a small green frog peeks out from under a lily pad.

And when that small green frog peeks out from under that lily pad, it sees an old raccoon sniffing along the pond bank, looking for something to eat.

And when that old raccoon climbs over the trunk of a fallen cottonwood tree, it sees a deer drinking from the moon-lit water.

And when that deer walks back up across the meadow, it sees an owl flying toward an old red barn on the other side of a field.

And when that owl lands on the open haymow door of that
old barn, it sees a farmer climbing down from the seat of a
great green tractor.

And when that farmer crosses the barnyard on his way back to the house, he sees a man in a rusty pickup truck driving down the dusty gravel road.

And when that man in the pickup truck pulls in to a gas station out on the highway, he sees a man in a huge silver eighteen-wheeler coming to a stop at a red light.

And when that truck driver passes beneath a railroad bridge, he sees a man in the window of a caboose at the end of a long freight train.

And when that man in the caboose passes through the next town, he sees a man walking his dog along a darkened street of small stores and shops.

And when that man with the dog comes to the next corner,
he sees a woman in a blue car come to a stop at a stop sign.

And when that woman in the blue car crosses the tracks and turns onto a quiet, tree-lined street, she sees a cat out walking across the grass.

And when that cat passes by a rosebush at the side of a
house, it sees a snow white moth flutter up to the light
coming from an upstairs window.

And when that snow white moth lands on the screen of that lighted window, it sees a young child lying in a cozy bed and a person who loves that child reading that child a storybook.

And when that person who loves that child turns the last page in that storybook, that person leans over and gives that child a kiss good night.

"Good night!"